MW01114013

TONY IS A HERO

by Lynda Bulla

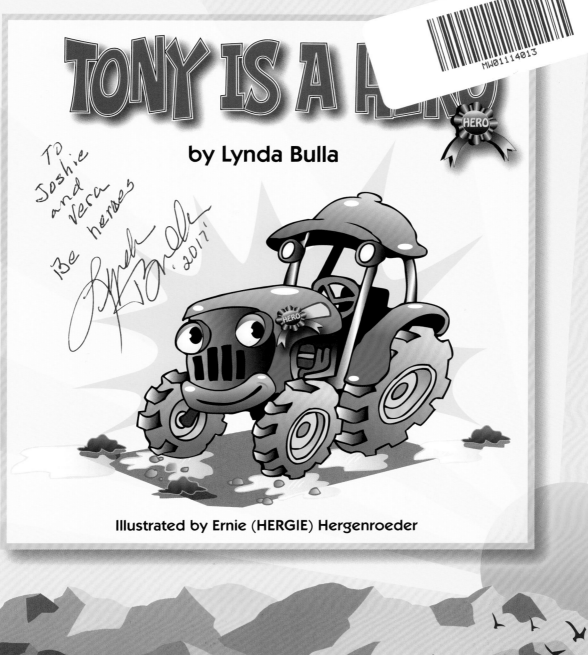

To
Joshie
and
Vera
Be heroes
Lynda Bulla
2017

Illustrated by Ernie (HERGIE) Hergenroeder

Tony was a tractor who lived on a farm.
He wasn't as big as the other tractors
that lived with him.
He was green, with big knobby tires
and two shiny lights on top.

He didn't have the size and power of Reggie who could pull a plow or make furrows for planting. He wasn't a track layer like Brutus who was the biggest and strongest of the tractors on the farm.

Brutus and Reggie loved to tease Tony
as he would go off to work.
**"Hey, pipsqueak,
don't get your tires dirty."**
Yeah, leave the big jobs
for someone who can handle them.

It was fun to see the crops of cotton, cantaloupe, corn or tomatoes sprouting through the crumbly soil every spring. Tony helped to grow the crops that fed lots of people around the world. His farmer grew lots of different crops. Each crop needed different care and Tony's work was important to a good harvest.

7

He loved to work among the almond trees
where it was shady, flattening the ground and
scraping away the unwanted weeds.
In the spring, the almond trees would bloom
with pretty pink flowers, and each fall Tony
would pull the trailer behind the sweeper that
picked the nuts off the ground and blew them
into the trailer. He loved the sound of the nut
hulls that crunched under his tires as he
helped in the harvest.

Tony was always very careful of the bunnies and ground squirrels that lived near the canal bank next to the orchard.
The canal brought water to the crops and supplied food and drink for all kinds of wildlife.

Large gray and white Sandhill cranes lived and nested among the tall reeds. Coyotes dug their den at the base of the old scraggily tree that grew near the canal. Hawks and eagles perched on the tall utility poles that marched proudly down the roads that crisscrossed the fields stretching as far as the eye could see.

Tony had a secret that he had never told anyone. He wanted more than anything to be a sports car.

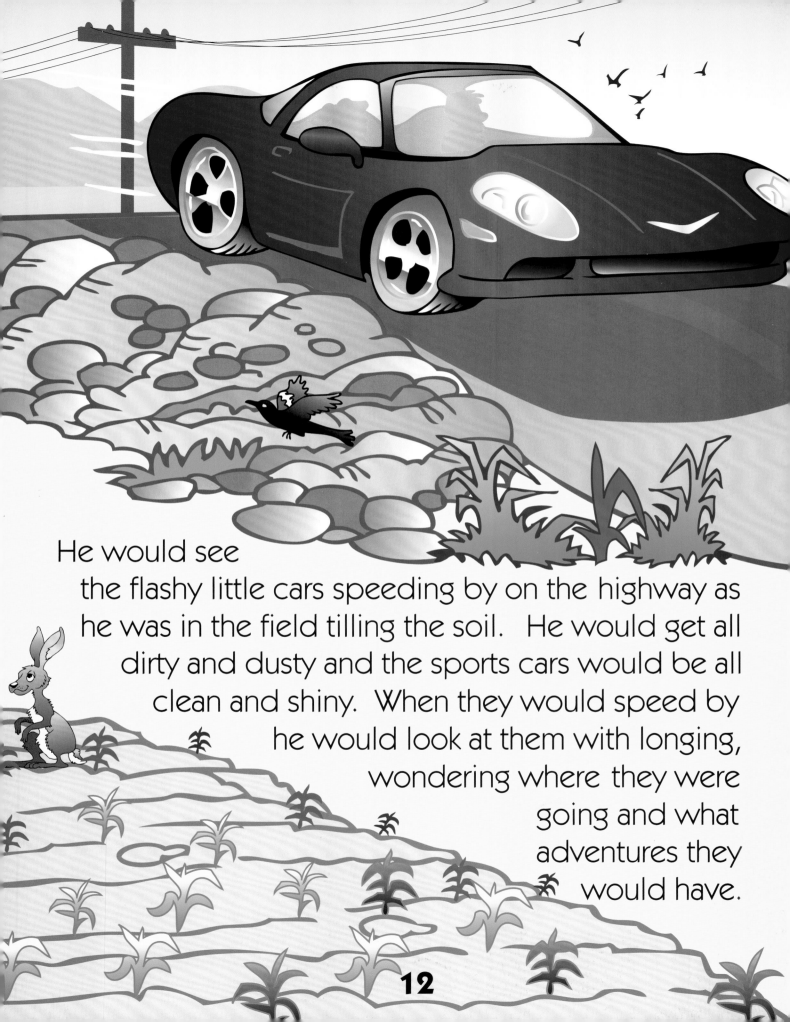

He would see
the flashy little cars speeding by on the highway as
he was in the field tilling the soil. He would get all
dirty and dusty and the sports cars would be all
clean and shiny. When they would speed by
he would look at them with longing,
wondering where they were
going and what
adventures they
would have.

That night, in the barn, as Tony thought about it, he became more and more unhappy. "Back and forth, that's all I ever do.

I know I could be a really good sports car, but I'm stuck on this farm and in the fields day after day. Why couldn't I have been a sports car instead of a stupid old tractor. I don't do anything exciting."

One day when Tony was scraping the weeds
from a big almond orchard by the highway,
he saw a bright red sports car pull into the
outside lane. All of a sudden,
he heard a loud **"POP"** and the sports car
went flying over the edge of the road and
landed on its side in the muddy irrigation ditch.

"Oh my," said Tony.

"We better go see if anyone needs help."
Tony shifted into high gear and went across the field
in record time, stirring up a big cloud
of dust behind him. When they arrived, there was
the car with its wheels spinning in the air.
One of the tires was flat.

"Help us," said a voice from inside the car. "We're stuck and we can't get out."

Tony was frightened. He started to huff and puff black smoke trying to figure out what to do. The policeman there looked over the problem. "We need to get them out of there," he said.

The farmer brought out a big chain, then he
unhooked Tony from the scraper blade,
and hooked the chain to the car and Tony's hitch.
**"Pull Tony" said the policeman.
"Pull as hard as you can!"**

Tony pulled, slowly and carefully,
while the man inside the car steered it,
the policeman guided Tony out of the ditch.
Soon the car was back on its wheels.

A young girl and a man crawled out of the wrecked car, muddy but otherwise unhurt. "Thank you for helping us" said the man. The farmer said, "Thank Tony. He was the one who was able to get you back on four wheels."

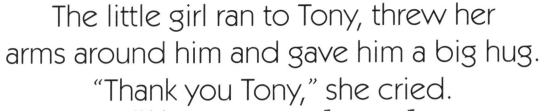

The little girl ran to Tony, threw her
arms around him and gave him a big hug.
"Thank you Tony," she cried.
**"You are a hero!
You saved us,"** she said.

Tony felt so good he smiled
and puffed white smoke.
"I am so glad I'm a tractor and
able to help," he thought.
"I'll never want to be a sports car again.
I'm happy being me."

That evening, back at the barn,
Brutus gave Tony a tractor high five by blowing
5 puffs of white smoke and saying "That was good kid.
You did a really good thing."

"Yeah" said Reggie, "I couldn't have
done it better myself.
Guess you're not a
pipsqueak anymore."

The farmer gave Tony a real good wash
to get off the mud, and painted a hero's
badge on the side of the grill,
to remind everyone that
Tony is a hero.